The (

Written by Jill Eggleton
Illustrated by Kelvin Hawley

Rigby

The **big** cats went to the cat show.

3

The little cats went to the cat show.

5

The **big** dog went to the cat show.

The **big** cats went under the table.

Big cats

The little cats went Meooowww!

Little cats

The **big** dog went out the door!

13

Labels

Little cats

Fat cats

Striped cats

Ginger cats

Black cats

Big cats

Guide Notes

Title: The Cat Show
Stage: Emergent – Magenta

Genre: Fiction
Approach: Guided Reading
Processes: Thinking Critically, Exploring Language, Processing Information
Written and Visual Focus: Labels
Word Count: 43

READING THE TEXT

Tell the children that the story is about a dog that visits a cat show.
Talk to them about what is on the front cover. Read the title and the author / illustrator.
"Walk" through the book, focusing on the illustrations and talking to the children about the different cats and what is happening on each page.
Before looking at pages 12 - 13, ask the children to make a prediction.
Read the text together.

THINKING CRITICALLY
(sample questions)
- Why do you think the dog went to the cat show?
- Why do you think the little cats weren't frightened of the dog?

EXPLORING LANGUAGE
(ideas for selection)

Terminology
Title, cover, author, illustrator, illustrations

Vocabulary
Interest words: cat, show, dog, table, meow, door
High-frequency words: the, went, to
Positional words: under, out

Print Conventions
Capital letter for sentence beginnings, periods